GUIDED MEDITATION SLEEP S

FOR CHILDREN

Book II

Welcome to these individual stories that are as individual as you!

Well I hope you enjoyed my first book putting your very own magic into it too, let's continue

the magic once again!

Linda Owen

First published in 2023 by Blossom Spring Publishing
Guided Meditation Sleep Stories for Children Book II © 2023 Linda Owen
ISBN 978-1-7392326-6-5
E: admin@blossomspringpublishing.com
W: www.blossomspringpublishing.com

Welcome to book II

About this book

Read each story together

Draw and colour me a picture to go with each individual story at the very end

Fall to sleep listening to each individual story again

Fill in the journal too about you!

Also by Linda Owen

GUIDED MEDITATION SLEEP STORIES FOR CHILDREN
25 MAGICAL STORIES – BOOK 1

DEDICATION

To all the children who love stories and those encouraged or introduced to them. Amongst my meditation work for adults it is an extra delight to address children's needs when it's time to entersleep - that passage through the night. I hope these stories are of great comfort and inspire your positive imagination that's simply magical!

Did you know kids whose mothers and fathers read to them are proven to handle entering school life better with less aggression or inattention such as ADHD. You are also creating a safe place to feel loved and valued in a world that is ever changing.

If you read slowly pausing with this script allowing a positive imagination with their breathing too will help them settle and we are creating a good bedtime routine to sustain a healthy mind and body.

These stories are also in audio style on Insight Timer with me plus I have many more for adults too.

Thank you xx

GUIDED MEDITATION SLEEP STORIES FOR CHILDREN

Are you ready to be read to by a parent or a trusted friend? Here is teamwork for each story is read at a steady pace whilst you the little listener close your eyes and imagine it all. By the time the story is complete it will lead you into pleasant dreams and going to bed will be magic!

Don't forget the other activities in this book too xx

Share your experience leave a book review on Amazon and thank you from me to you xx

CONTENTS BOOK TWO

Welcome to Camp Kids Meditation

Welcome to a virtual camping holiday done in style

To lift your mood and rid any stress

Let's begin

Please lie down or get comfy in a chair

Get really comfy

Please close just one eye shut

And please close the other eye shut

It begins with an early rise

For the camping holiday will very much

Be observing nature too

So listen out for a hoot or two coming outside the home

There's a camping van pulling up outside your very home

There are 5 things in that camping van

The driver of the camper van grandpa Mr Holiday

And grandma Mrs Holiday with her home baked cookies

There is also one old dog called Scinder with his old pal

An old cat called Earl

They grew up together

Because Mrs Holiday wanted a dog and Mr Holiday wanted a cat

And the fifth is a baby chick that fell out of its tree

That is being looked after for a couple of weeks

So once again grab your backpack

And super quick saying goodbye and see you all again in a week

Then run out of the home

For grandpa is already started the camper van up

Up the step with a big jump and slide that door

Looking around inside and noticing how settled everyone is

Lots of room here with grandpa singing to the country radio

And grandma with her flask of tea and cookies for everyone

The old dog is sleeping

The cat is dreaming away for its tail is twitching

And the baby bird is lovely and warm in a dark straw box

With a timer on the side for feeding times, of course

So settle down on a lovely hand-knitted blanket

Feel as if you've seen this blanket before

For some things are made to last

And get passed down the family - maybe it smells of good memories

A journey, a drive on the steady lane for there is scenery to be enjoyed

Getting there to the campsite you may nibble a cookie or maybe have a drink or take a snooze

And you might wake up shortly to find the dog Scinder

And the cat Earl have crept up and slept beside you

Simply because they love their holiday visitor

So settle down here for a full minute…

What a cosy camper it is

And the sunshine has got brighter along that road and has wakened up all sleepy heads

Listen carefully for the bird buzzer will go off

In the next 20 seconds

Watch grandma open a tub of worms and prepare little chick's breakfast

Grandpa announces we are arriving on camp

And winds down his window to pay for a pitch

And grabs a map of where they will be putting the old van

Right then

It's time to turn the camping van into a full kitted out tent

So roll up the sleeves get ready for instructions

For helping hands make light work plus

You'll need to fix the gas bottle, the water tank

And plug into the electrics

I shall leave you here for a full minute to make it gorgeous

It's been decided your new duty is feeding chick, the baby bird

So grandpa hands over his special watch timer to keep in your pocket

It usually goes off every 3 hours

We need now camp firewood for we always sit around a campfire once the sun goes down

So let's all go for a walk about and forage for loose dead wood on this beautiful forest campsite

And shall leave you here a full minute to bring it back to the van...

Keeping it tidy, see the bundles of dead wood, enough for a week laid nearby the camp doors

Now there is a sense of freshening up

So what would be better than a lake and a swim in it

Start to follow the old dog Scinder

Who's been a regular here, for he too loves the camp lake

And of course grandparents are super swimmers steady of course

Just need to take the picnic hamper, some towels

The usual stuff and safety floats if you wish

So start to picture this for a full minute...

Grandpa is extremely brave and extravagant as he turns almost into a dot

For he swims in long straight lines

But turns around eventually, back in time for that picnic

Describe to yourself this perfect lake

Are there fish or frogs? Ducks and ducklings?

Maybe geese? Is it very cool in it? Can you see the bottom?

Explore, remember lakes are like mirrors and trees and clouds

Will reflect into it, stay with this for a full minute...

Ready for a juicy apple and then a sandwich and a slice of homemade cake

Which one do you like?

Now grandma is very much a bird fancier, a bird watcher

And announces each morning we are up with the birds and will observe them all for a good hour

Plus little chick will enjoy this very much and needs to see the action

Sometimes the evening campfire seems to be the best thing at the end of the day

A chance for a good chat and natter with the grandparents

And hear some tales too

Plus the dog Scinder and the cat Earl love a campfire

So once you've fed the baby chick under grandma's watchful eye

Of which I will leave you here for a minute...

Now two guitars old style are brought out of the camper van

And a little lesson is given to help you learn it

Grandpa says, close your eyes and feel this instrument, all of it

So you do and I shall leave you a minute to explore this guitar

Learning a short simple guitar song is a good step in the right direction

So feel you are guided by grandpa, for a tune will be made

And I shall leave you here for a minute to do this...

It's time grandma told you a camp story

So wrap yourself in that lovely, knitted blanket that smells of good things

She clears her throat and begins

Once upon a time, a real tribe couple was spotted

In the deep woods of this very camp site, this was 40 years ago

When grandpa and I were very much younger

Enough to really walk our legs off, like explorers

And enjoyed going off the beaten track

That day we went for hours, up early, of course

We found indeed a tiny waterfall with unusual rocks around it

With markings of forest animals and symbols of stars on many rocks

We knew they weren't by no means the sort of a regular person would have done

We began to tread very carefully for a cave entrance so very small indeed

Looked like someone was living in it

That day we kept an eye on the time and left a small present

Nothing much, just a couple of tin mugs

And walked back home singing as usual

Well, curiosity got the better of us

And once more we went on that big walk very early

And just as we felt we were in the right place, a complete blocked path was there

Made from big boulders of wood

But we sighted in a way a gift, for the 2 tin mugs had been replaced

With 2 wooden charms - one was an owl and one a flute

We decided to respect their privacy and returned home

But that night we both had the same amazing dream

In that very dream we talked about it the next morning

How we met 2 real tribal people both were a couple

They looked very wild and fresh and full of life

The woman had jet black hair down to her waist

And the man had long hair tied in a ponytail

They said the tokens of the owl and flute are lucky

And will bring much happy news through life

And thanked us for respecting their privacy

They liked that grandma loved birds

And grandpa could play the guitar

By now everyone was fast asleep continuing the dream story

For they all wanted a visit from the tribal couple too

And learn how they in a way camp outdoors all the time

Even their love for the bees and honey was eaten

And also a medicine in a way

A few hours later, the alarm goes off to feed the baby chick

And so you must attend to it

So take this moment here

Looking deep into those little chick's eyes and aware how light for flying it is

And so we come back to you as well, as the chick looks back at you

For it's really time for you to come back right to the beginning of this story

Where you were at home

So at the count of 10

If you wish to fully awake or if not then continue with

The holiday and turn off now if you wish

Or just continue to listen to me

Let's bring back awake at home fully refreshed and happy

From that camping holiday

Counting to 10

1 2 3 4 5 6 7 8 9 10

Time to open your eyes, fully open the eyes

Eyes wide open feeling fresh and happy

Thank you

DRAW WHAT YOU SAW

IN **CAMP KIDS MEDITATION**

LION IN YOUR HEART

Welcome to this 5 minute, **Lion in Your Heart** meditation

Let's stand please and have one full stretch right now

Now bring your posture into a strong standing position

Please close your eyes

Chin slightly up with a rise in the chest

Locate your heart within your mind

And the lion in your heart

The inner strength, the leader

The power, you shine out

Imagine, the image of a lion in your heart

Recognise its colours

Its body shape

Its mane and its tail

Think about the eyes

And think of the sound a lion does make

For the roar of a lion, can be heard a mile away

See the complete image, in your heart

Representing the inner strength, the leader

The power, you shine out

Name this lion after your full name

By saying it, inside your mind right now

Now let the image of your lion

With each breath grow in size

So please inhale fully now and hold 5 seconds

Then release it and see the lion grow twice as big

Inhale fully again and hold 5 seconds

Then release it and see the lion grow twice as big

Inhale fully holding 5 seconds

And release it and see the lion twice as big now

Then inhale fully and hold 5 seconds

Then release it and see the lion - it's perfect, fully grown size

Now, picture both of you

Standing on a diamond platform, of abundant bright energy

Feel a radiant glow, throwing upwards lighting you both up

Ready to walk proudly

The inner strength, the leader

The power you shine out

Say thank you to your lion, with your name

At the count of 4

To opening the eyes, the eyes of a lion

1 2 3 4

Eyes wide open

Thank you

DRAW WHAT YOU SAW

IN **LION IN YOUR HEART**

Welcome to this guided meditation called

Fast to Sleep with My Unicorn

Let's begin

Ready for bedtime

In your bedroom

On your bed

Please squeeze your pillow now

To make it dreamy and fluffy

Get comfortable into bed

Closing 1 eye to sleep

Closing the next eye to dream of unicorns

Now

Before your personal unicorn enters the bedroom

Think how much you really like unicorns

Smile, feel that smile

For they are strong, happy and magical

It would be nice to give this unicorn a name

Think of a name to call your unicorn

So please, let a name pop in your head

Yes, a personal name for your unicorn

Good

Because unicorns are so super bright

And because it really is bedtime

This unicorn, like magic, will shrink to a tiny size

No bigger than your hand

Yes, just the right size for bedtime

So smile, feel that smile

So please invite your tiny

But perfect unicorn into your bedroom

By saying their name over and over

Listen and feel the magic begin

As your unicorn sneaks into your bedroom

Like a small glowing white bubble

The size of your hand

This bright, tiny unicorn

Little sound of horse hooves

Such happiness, is entering your bedroom

With those flying wings

Your unicorn can easily get on your bed

And immediately puts his bright unicorn face close to your head

To say hello and I am here for bedtime dreaming

He's training you up, of course

To think great thoughts and great feeling about yourself

To make you strong, bright and happy, of course

Yes, collect all the magical bits from each day

Every day is touched by unicorn happiness

To have days full of greatness and goodness

He starts to strut

Up and down your bed

Prancing up and down your bed

Getting ready to do some fast galloping and jumping over obstacles

Then he asks

To enter inside of you, to chase out any heaviness

So you can become lighter, yet stronger

With a yes from you, nod your head, good

He leaps onto your heart

Then gallops, snorting and goes all around the body

Leaving a trail of magic sparkle light behind him

He's chucking out anything that's sad and boring

Leaving only unicorn silvery white sparkles

So listen and feel

Everything changing inside

Getting crazy sparkly super bright

To lightness and sheer strength

Now he knows it's bedtime

And comes now to settle on your pillow

So together, resting now, deeply into your pillow

Both to fall asleep

For dreams are to be made

Getting ready, for magical dreams

It's nearly time

Time to let your unicorn become a full size unicorn once more

To enter your new dream

As your pillow too, melts into sheer dreamy lightness

Time to really start a new adventure and explore together

And jump on his back and fly into dreams

Remember, nothing gets in the way of a unicorn

They are so bright they light everything up

Hold on tight

Give a tiny kiss, full of love and full of laughter onto your unicorn

Get ready to fly, to gallop, to run wild and free

Into the biggest, most colourful of dreams

So at the count of 7, enter the dream tunnel

1 2 3 4 5 6 7

Superfast, to sleep

Superfast, dreaming big

Colourful dreams, high together

Keep those dreams colourful, together

Together

With my unicorn

So wishing and blessing

You both a fantastic dream

DRAW WHAT YOU SAW

IN **FAST TO SLEEP WITH MY UNICORN**

WORRY IS ALWAYS IN A HURRY

Welcome to this guided meditation story

Called **Worry Is Always in a Hurry**

Let's begin

Please be seated or relax, lie down if you wish

Closing one eye thank you

Closing the next eye thank you

Let the eyes inside

Go up and down, up and down

Let the eyes inside go side to side, side to side

Then stop, time to begin

To really understand worry

Let's begin

The star of the show is, worry

So the question is

Why is he?

The fear of worry

Or is it?

Fear thinking

Overthinking on worry

I love this questions and answer

Question, are you worried?

Answer, would it help?

No!

Worry is always in a hurry

Where are you going?

To the worry head department

Stop!

Slow down, right here

Time to put a smile on that face

Feel that smile, getting bigger and bigger than worry

Cheeks riding high

Eyes are squinting and blinking and sparkling

So chin up and look for the answer

Roll up the sleeves

Learn to laugh and lift a new way, out of it

Look at it differently

Stop fear thinking

Turning a molehill into a mountain

Step back to that molehill

For molehills belong in the ground

Lots of pats on the back, each step well done me

Learn to be inspired

Everyone likes a hero or a happy ending for sure

Going nowhere really, is worry

Let's go back to basics, logic

Emotions, keep lifting them

My happy emotional rewards

Yes, like a story and a good ending

We all have a sense of humour, use it skilfully

There's always someone doing better

But I feel, this is a bit of magic really

To keep you going and reaching high, achieving in life

Celebrating, now that calls for a party

Should I keep a diary of me, stamping out worry?

Mummy explains, worry is a bit like change

Worry, dances around changes

Here's a story about worry

This little girl Francesca, said this

I'm late, yes, I'm late to see my friend Julie

I should have been there by now

The clock looked at her, wagging its finger

You're late!

Mummy said, "OK, let's go now"

"But I'm late"

Is all Francesca could think

Mummy said, "Sorry there's been extra chores today so let's be on our way"

Stepping out together, it's just a 20 minute walk

But how Francesca did worry every step

Worry got louder in her ears, listening to it in her head

But mummy was smiling, and enjoyed the fresh air walk

Taking in the sights of springtime, of pink blossom on all the trees

Looking at everyone's front garden, down the streets

But Francesca didn't like being late

She doesn't like letting friends down

What would they say?

So she began to frown

Her face, lost its smile

She couldn't see the pink blossom trees

That only blossom once a year

Her head lowered, looking at the ground

But when they both got there

Francesca explained to her friend Julie, "Why I am late"

She picked her up and tickled her

"It's OK, it's OK", said Julie

"I knew you were coming

So that was good enough for me"

Francesca began to smile

And could really feel that smile

So she decided, the next time to be careful, not to worry so much

"I think I'll swap it to be a little happy", she said to her head

"For a little happy, is my personality shining through

And it would be nice, to see the pink blossom trees

And all the different gardens and breathe deeply the fresh air"

So being happy, is her new strength

And she learnt that today

And thanked Mr Worry, for showing her the way

Because it's OK, it's OK

Francesca learnt that she can be the master of worry

Be more like mum, keep her chin up

So worry pointed at a problem

Or is it about little changes?

Changes, challenges and how strong are you

Building those happy muscles

So back to that question, are you worried?

And the answer, would it help?

No!

And that's the end of Mr Worry

And the beginning of the happy you

Thank you

Time to open your eyes now

And be a little happy too

DRAW WHAT YOU SAW

IN **WORRY IS ALWAYS IN A HURRY**

PIRATES AT THE SEASIDE

Welcome to this guided story meditation

Called **Pirates at the Seaside**

Are you ready?

Seated or lie down if you wish

Listening with your eyes closed

A day at the seaside with my twin

And at the seashore, where rides upon a pirate ship

Looking like it came out of a fairy tale

Now much later in life, for life is a story

For who would have thought that just me

Would travel so far from home

Where I would see a familiar pirate ship in the faraway land of Hong Kong?

The Chinese junk boats, with a special one on the harbour

For tourists of course, has most definitely a pirate look about it

Such beautiful curves and shapes and colours and flags

Sails like a colourful picture

Did you know

The Chinese junk boat is one of the most successful types of sailing ships in history

First developed in 220 BCE

They could carry up to 700 passengers

And often carried goods from Africa and India

And sailors hung red flags to please dragons

They believed lived in the sea

But back to the beginning, as a little child with my twin

28

Who has loved anything to do with pirates

"Why?

Why do you like pirates so much, Wendy?"

Her eyes lit up, but I still remained puzzled

"All that beautiful treasure", she said

"All pirates have a treasure chest

No time to be boring, every day is different

For sailors at sea, sailing to new places

Islands to be discovered

Battles to be won

Their love for parrots, the talking ones, of course

And clever monkeys, that the captain really loves

A bottle of rum and singing their songs

Out on the big, big, open sea

Through all kinds of weather

A storm would brew and all the crew

With all their muscles, set all their sails

And play with the wind

For ships can travel fast and forwards. with gales behind its wings

Tattoos on skin, from exotic places they've been

Stories at night, some would give you a fright

Superstition, luck was essential

Casting good luck spells and lucky habits

Land and sea, a wonderful life, that's the ticket

Life ever changing

Always something new to see

Finding new plants and new animals, where faraway places are found by sea

Meeting new people that speak a different tongue

Lots of healthy sea air, sunshine, brown and tanned

Sea legs and swimming with dolphins

Eating fish every night

Collecting pearls from oysters galore

It's a wonderful life, to be a pirate in this colourful world

They cover every corner of this world

No stone left unturned

They write down all their news, in the captain's book, like a diary

And a book of knowledge, all kept on ship

In their treasure chest, marking history as they go

They buy, they sell, bargain and swap

They are strong and can see right into your soul,"

Said Wendy, looking deeply into my eyes

"They speak many languages when they stay, here and there

They do not worry, but happy to be alive

And love the captain, his wise old head

And all true friends, looking after each other

So pirates are the heroes and explorers of this great world

And have seen it all, what a wonderful life

And that's why I love everything about pirates

What a life, what a ball."

Thank you for listening, to why my twin Wendy loves pirates

The end of this story

Time to open your eyes and explore the world around you, me thinks

DRAW WHAT YOU SAW

IN **PIRATES AT THE SEASIDE**

LOST AND FOUND

Welcome to this guided meditation story

Called **Lost and Found**

Let's begin

Please get seated or lie down if you wish

Closing one eye for lost thank you

Closing the next eye for found

Let the eyes inside go up and down up and down

For something is lost

Then let the eyes inside go side to side, side to side

For something shall be found again

Settle down and listen to this story

Now where have I put my colouring book?

I had it yesterday

All day long

How I love my colouring book

But this day, something has gone wrong

I have looked in all the places I go

In my bedroom

On the settee

Did I put it in my school bag?

Or In a drawer perhaps

So I take a deep breath in

And I put my detective thinking cap on

I caught myself in the mirror

And asked, with eyes that looked back at me

"Where is it, show me?"

Think, think, like a detective let's turn it into a game

Be a little super-duper detective

And trace your moves of yesterday

I took a deep breath in

My eyes rolled up, looking at my thinking detective head

Well I got out of bed, check

Dressed in a hurry, check

Bathroom brushing teeth, check

It was a Saturday, not a school day, check

My friend Amy came round to play in the back yard

She brought her colouring book too

When it started raining, we stayed outside, laughing at the rain drops and puddles

Then we came in and settled at the table to colour in our books

We shared the crayons because together, we had more colours to choose

Amy's parents arrived to take her home

The dog Benji, jumped up at the table

And knocked my colouring book to the floor

It had a tear

So mummy said, she would put some sticky tape on it

When she gets to grandma's, later that day

So mum took my book

Yes, now I remember

She took my book but when she got back

Mum had so much shopping and things to say

That my colouring book had been all forgotten

Mum had forgotten to give my colouring book back to me

So I asked my mum

And she did reply, it's still in the car

Grandma mended it for you

And she's even put a cover over it, to protect it

With a picture of you 2 on it

Shall I get it?

Yes, please and thank you very much

And that is how

I lost and found my colouring book

So good luck, to your detective thinking head

The end of this story

Thank you

Open eyes 1 2 3

DRAW WHAT YOU SAW

IN **LOST AND FOUND**

TINY TEDDY MY BIG COMFORT

Welcome to this guided meditation

Called **Tiny Teddy My Big Comfort**

Please get seated or lie down if you wish

Let's begin

Closing one eye to relax

Closing the next eye to imagine

The story begins

The tiny teddy, my big comfort

It was a present

Bought at the seaside

To go with my other toys

But tiny teddy has such a cheeky smile

Lovely eyes

And just the right size to go everywhere with me

Or at least, this is what I found out

Sometimes I get nervous, or is it just too much pressure at times?

So tiny teddy whispers in my ear

"Bring me along, I'll show you how to make things lighter and fun"

At first teddy stayed in just one room

But he is light and hand size, just the right size, yes

Right size on my laptop

And when in the car

He sits on my lap with safety seat belt, across us both

And in traffic jams I squeeze his paws, for deep comfort

My bag has many pockets on the outside, like for my water bottle

But teddy has made space for himself

I've started making cool outfits for him too

It doesn't take much, a bit of this, a bit of that

In fact it's usually lightning fast

I remember taking him to the Viking Festival

So first I dressed myself up, like a Viking of course

And tiny teddy, he was all kitted out

He was very popular, for no other toy looked like a Viking

With armour and shield and all the other kids did squeal

Then Lola, a family friend, took tiny teddy back to her campervan

I knew he'd gone missing, as I saw on the grass his Viking shield all on its own

But Lola had fun and I guess tiny teddy did too

Holidays were pretty cool, off he goes, making a journey, suddenly an adventure

His eyes are popping at all the sights

For it's great to simply get out and about, into the big wide world

Wherever we stop, he jumps on the bed and claims his pillow for his tiny soft head

He sits on the settee when the TV is on

And watches too all the football, cheering them on

He moves to music for he's quite a dancing bear

He's a great dancer, from hard rock to sweet melodies

He has a big mouth, leadership and bossing the bigger toys about

I can't complain really, everyone is busy

But teddy is there for comfort and care

He truly is my big, big comfort

I love you, teddy bear

I love you very, very much

The end and wakey wakey if you please

DRAW WHAT YOU SAW

IN TINY TEDDY MY BIG COMFORT

BREATHING INTO MY BALLOON PARTY

Welcome to this guided story meditation called

Breathing Into My Balloon Party

Let's begin

Please lie down fully

For the fun to begin

Closing one eye to get ready

Closing the next eye for balloons

Let the eyes inside now go up and side to side

Then let the eyes inside, go down and side to side

Then eyes ready

And focused on being in charge of this balloon party

Imagine the ceiling above you is waiting for a delivery of balloons

The balloons need your help

They need the support of your life breath

They require you to blow them up with your breathing

So simply imagine an invisible brand new balloon

Drops from the ceiling onto your belly

It simply hasn't any colour

So help this poor balloon to fully, magically, come alive

The new invisible balloon is the size of your hand

And asks you to place it under your lip and blow out a long breath

But wait, it wants to be super red

So nearly ready

Rest the other hand on your tummy

And the other hand with the brand new balloon

Just under your lips, and blow a full breath out into it

Believe this little balloon

Is beginning to grow quickly into a bright red balloon

Ready to tie it and then tell it

To float about above you in your room

Get ready for the next invisible balloon to drop on your tummy

It is as big as your hand and wants blowing up, too

Bring the new balloon just under your lip and blow out a long breath

But wait, it wants to be orange and yellow

Resting the other hand on your tummy

Helps to feel the power of your magic breath

Blow a long breath out and believe the balloon

Is beginning to grow very quickly into an orange and yellow balloon

Just another deep breath and blow it again

And now it's just the right size of a lovely orange and yellow balloon

Ready to tie and tell it to float about just above you in your room

Let's do two more balloons, then move onto some more fun with them

So the next invisible new balloon drops on your tummy, the size of your hand

Remember what to do, bring just under the lip

Rest other hand on tummy

This balloon would like to be green at the top, with blue in the middle

And purple at the bottom

Blow a long breath and believe, this new balloon is getting bigger

With green, then blue, then purple

Just one more breath, to fill it up to the right size

Ready to tie it up and tell this colourful balloon

To rise up, floating about above you in this room

Now the last balloon will be you!

Now to say thank you, all the colourful balloons would like

To take you for a float about with them

And simply have a balloon party, dancing around the ceiling of course

So decide what colour you would like to change into

Begin to notice your big breath breathing in is the one that's changing you

Another deep breath in, getting a good size to rise

Take through your nose a deep breath in, to finish making you as light as air

Imagine tying up yourself, to keep super light

Then wish yourself to rise up and join the colourful balloons

Then have a full minute, sixty seconds bouncing in the air all together

And sing a party song if you wish, or simply dance in the air

Just do what balloons do best, enjoy this and see you in one minute

Now see yourself, taking all your colourful balloons

With you in front, floating outdoors, out of this room

Watch them happily follow you, like balloon party friends

And a very nice wind, so quickly, picks all of you and whisks you away

So fast, so high, all of you

Suddenly miles and miles, far away

And the higher you all go the lighter you all feel

Now for fun, find the nearest fluffiest white cloud and claim it

By putting yourselves on top of it

Feel the magic of air and your breath, the wind, this white fluffy cloud

And your balloon friends, all of you in wonderful colours

Just like a rainbow in the sky

The sky is so light, so big

Then tell this lovely white fluffy cloud

To bring you all back home, in ten seconds

Super, fast now 1 2 3 4 5 6 7 8 9 10

Back in that room, big smile

Now clap your hands three times, now

Thank you

Time to open your beautiful eyes

DRAW WHAT YOU SAW

IN **BREATHING INTO MY BALLOON PARTY**

WINTER CASTLE WALLS

Welcome to this meditation sleep story called

Winter Castle Walls

Let's begin

Please jump on your bed and squeeze your pillow

Please make it nice and fluffy

Get comfortable, into bed now

Rest your head into that fluffy pillow

Closing one eye for winter

Closing the next eye for castle walls

Let's begin

It was another day within the castle walls, for the two of them

Yes, most castles

No sorry, all castles have amazing secrets

Hidden rooms, escape tunnels, a place to live beneath the castle

And all around it, huge, tall walls

There was a time castles held battles, to protect their bounties of treasure

And because they are built to last

They soon become hundreds and hundreds and hundreds of years old

What great architecture, designed to perfection

A place for the wealthy, the famous, the high society

But back to those winter castle walls

They were never, ever, used in winter

For fear of the whole thing crumbling, for castles have feelings

Wooden doors got stiffer, door handles were chilly to turn

So as winter sleeps so does the castle, a little

Or maybe not, clever travellers, experts in castle secret dwellings

Passed down from a close clan

Dean was one of them, being the adventurous traveller

Dean and his lucky friend, the ginger tomcat

Every winter they both stopped their travels of the outdoor life

And took free lodgings, in their chosen castle

Sometimes it was Scotland, even France

Anywhere really

The secret information was carried down from secret travellers

And for luck they always had a ginger tomcat

What they were doing was quite unique, and simply great for the world and the environment

For travellers, the wandering type, were in tune with how the world

Mother Earth herself, recycles naturally

And castles are known for their extravagant, super rich, indulging over the top the best of everything

And with everything, there was a lot of leftovers, like too much food for example

Well, one would expect to dine like a king or queen every night

But too much food, plus you weren't supposed to eat everything on your plate

So delicious foods, were put down the waste chute in the castle walls

Heading for the bin

Or maybe not, with hungry Dean and hungry ginger tomcat

By the time winter had come and gone, they both put a fair bit of weight on

Water was a laugh too, for they could hear the staff running the water

To a desired temperature and a desired level and clarity clean

So down the plug hole, down the chute, water unused

From a tap left running was filled into buckets by traveller Dean

Well ginger tomcat licked quickly, to satisfy his thirst

Dean put his lucky mug under and kettle and pan too

It wasn't a quiet castle either

Oh no, for that would never do

For fine music filled the air, it travelled from room to room

So loud each night, and a dance and a jig or a time to dream

The two did so, every night

Odd bits of furniture got thrown away

When it was no longer popular or needed repairing

But castles, like the best of the best

And down the chute, with a sound as clear as a bell

As Dean rushed to grab it

And marvelled at his new chair and table, that he repaired in a jiffy

Clothes at times got too tight for castle people

For putting weight on did happen from time to time, especially in winter

Then down the chute, a lovely set of clothes and even some boots

Ginger tomcat was hoping to get something a little more animal

And often dreamed of a nice cushion to curl up on and call his own

Then about four of the blooming things, went down the chute

A little faded but extra super soft, that called for a purr of delight

Toy things to play with, went down the chute too

Once they had become bored of them or were slightly broken

Now that was a good castle, surprise toys that Dean was gifted in repairing

Such as the spinning top and the wind-up musical mouse

Winter walls, winter days, and winter nights

Fires burning in most rooms, with logs and coal

And the heat, did warm the walls indeed

Sometimes, they held their feet against them and smiled at each other

Though a cat, always looks like it's smiling

By the end of winter, they were both keen to travel once more

So a quick tidy up, in case they would be back next year

Though visiting other castles was something they preferred

As Dean stroked the ginger tomcat making plans

And so happy gave out long purrs

A traveller sees so much more, for each day is new

Each night sky is a treasure, to the dreamy eyes before sleep

The seasons, the colours, the villages, different ways of life

Were a part of Dean's and ginger tomcat's travelling afar

Sometimes they found ancient treasures, in those hidden places of castle walls

So they always had a bit of money, to see each year in and out

But then again, they had made life their own, a world that gave something to talk about

Would you like to dream of castles?

And secretly have a ball in the castle walls

Think of winter, whispering in your ears

Winter

Let them take you, with a lucky ginger tomcat

To winter castle walls, let the two of you go and live in there

Dream castle and ginger tomcat

And remember to dream

Big

Good night from Dean and ginger tomcat

DRAW WHAT YOU SAW

IN WINTER CASTLE WALLS

OH MY GOODNESS

O.M.G.

Welcome to this guided sleep meditation

Called **Oh My Goodness O.M.G.**

Let's begin

Ready for bed

Find your pillow

Prepare your pillow

Please give it a mighty magic squeeze

For the best dreams ever

Please settle into bed now

And rest your head onto the soft pillow

Closing the right eye begin to

Tense the right side of the body, all your right muscles tight

Closing the left eye and

Tense the left side of the body, all your left muscles tight

Please completely relax that whole body now

Let's think and dream about something wonderful

Going back in time to the past

Possibly 80 years ago, almost, nearly, not quite a hundred years ago

Oh my goodness, O.M.G.

How your grandparents lived when they were children too

Before television, before computers and mobile phones, having a family car

Lots of things were yet to be invented

Back to the past and let's have a good look in this dream

Grandparents as children

So first, let's watch grandma stop growing older

But start looking younger, as she shrinks to child size

Look at her hair, all long and shiny in pony tails

Her cheeks are covered in freckles

And she starts giggling like a playful little girl

Her hands are the right size for your hands

In her pocket is a piece of magic string for hand string games

Remind her later to show you this game

That works well passing the string to one another

Let's watch grandpa stop growing old

And start looking younger, as he shrinks to child size

Look at his thick curly hair

Freckles on a little nose

Dainty, yet his arms have little muscles

Hands too, the right size for you

In his pocket, are shiny coloured glass marbles, to play and win with

Also a bit of an anytime, anywhere game

Which he can explain later in your dream

So, with everyone holding hands now, it's time

To skip out and head to the past

Almost, not quite, nearly a hundred years ago

Looking at their childhood homes

We know in a sense they both grew in different houses

But both would be very similar

So, there is a small front garden, but a big garden at the back

There are some chickens laying fresh eggs

And a tortoise freely roaming about in this garden

The tortoise is eating a fresh strawberry

Take a moment to look a little closer

As you follow the tortoise to the back of the garden

A much loved dog is here, with a hand painted kennel

Where he heads for cover on rainy days

There's an old ball chewed up nicely by this dog

And one football, one netball

I wonder, what your favourite dog is in the whole world?

Oh my goodness, O.M.G.

So many vegetables are growing and growing here

All in neat rows of different colours, for vegetables are very colourful

There is fruit, too, fresh strawberries

And a much loved apple tree for baking pies

There are quite a few bicycles of different sizes, for there is no car

Some of the bicycles have a basket on the front, for shopping trips

Yes, a long time ago some things were yet to be invented

So, no car, no television, no computers, no mobile phones

How did they balance work with play?

Time to look inside grandma's and grandpa's home

When they were children too

Let's open that front door

Notice inside the door

There's a row of wellington boots for lots of walkabouts

For all types of weather, be it rainy or snowy

And a kite or two for windy weather fun games

Have a moment, feel the lightness of colourful flying kites

A pair of old roller skates are hanging up

For they were too much trouble laid on the floor

Anyone could have had an accident

Hand knitted colourful really long scarves

For the seasons of autumn and winter

What colours would you have liked your own scarf to be knitted in?

Simply imagine now and hang it up in a jiffy!

Follow your noses into the kitchen if you please

The kitchen is like a busy bakery shop

With baking tins, glass jars and big pot bowls

To make dozens of cheap and cheerful homemade treats

Like jam tarts and sausage rolls

Can you smell the warm sweet toffee apples setting in the kitchen window?

Delicious smells and heat fill the kitchen air

So grab a warm toffee apple and keep walking and exploring about

Well, I really can't see any televisions

But there is a large old style radio with a lot of chairs

And a rocking chair and bean bags around the radio

The radio has a big button to switch it on and off

The button, if you look, is worn out a bit

So they must have loved listening to it

Now singing was big in most homes, too

Mum, dad, the children, all had great singing voices

Singing in the bath, the shower, singing whilst doing chores

Sing along to radio songs of course

There's a newspaper showing what time the radio programmes are on

Children's radio stories

Family stories that are on daily and some weekly

Sometimes listening is enough, for we can still imagine it all in the head

A long shiny wooden cabinet has many records on its shelves

And opens up in the middle to reveal a record player

So you would have to be a bit of a D.J.

And change the records of different songs yourself

Most of us like dancing and that includes me

Explore later what music you would like to hear

There's some cinema tickets for the weekend

Where big films were first seen on a large screen

By hundreds of children for the very first time together

Often an ice cream interval where the film stopped halfway

A lot of these films years later have been redone differently

But here will be the original great films

Also theatre tickets but not too many

Theatre shows with a big one at Christmas and some for public holidays

Also some small bus tickets when a long journey is too much by foot

For the public bus is fun and fast to get about

Now going upstairs, yes upstairs

Where bunkbeds fitted well in a small bedroom

Each bed has a hot water bottle to keep toes lovely and warm

Den making is a lot of fun too, throwing large blankets over a chair or 2

There are a few old toys that aided and created with other children pantomime stories

Old dolls, a few soldiers and really interesting teddy bears

And dressing-up clothes that often called for a visit to the parents' wardrobe

Once you asked permission to wear a hat or a different coat or a scarf

There are many board games and card games

For children and parents too can join in

Board games really last well and don't really wear out and no batteries

A game of dominoes, Monopoly, maybe you know some more

Colourful jigsaw puzzles paint a picture piece by piece

There are library members cards in a drawer to keep them tidy

So books galore could be borrowed from the local library

Books are really special full of things you like

And libraries keep every book you could possibly imagine

I'm going to finish now with a lovely long list

Of so many things for you all to continue in this dream

Yes, a list of things grandparents did as children

Little boys like frogs and snails

Little girls like flowers and ladybirds

Cinema tickets, wonderful new films

Radio stories daily and weekly

Singing voices fill the house with love

Pocket money

Big family jumble sales

The Brownies

The Scouts

School trips on a big bus

Gardens full of fresh vegetables

Pets at home - dogs, cats, fish and tortoises

Jigsaw puzzles galore

Board games and card games

Dancing to records

Acting pantomime, real pantomime

Roller skating, cycling long distances

Walkabouts and climbing trees

Dog shows

Vegetable shows, the biggest and the best

Home baking, den making

Chalk games with a hop and a skip

Drawing, colouring competitions

Instruments to play

Flying kites in the wind

Marbles to play and win

Books from the library

Charity shops full of treasure

Skipping ropes and boats to float

Sandcastle days

But no

No television, no computer, no phone, no car

No plastic was invented just yet

Tins, glass jars and large pot bowls

Please keep exploring and dreaming of grandpa and grandma's home

From the past

It's time for a very big yawn

Yawn, yawn, yawn

Rest into your soft pillow

For happy dreams

And dream again and again

Sweet dreams

DRAW WHAT YOU SAW

IN OH MY GOODNESS O.M.G.

RAINBOW POWER BODY AND
POWER ANIMAL SLEEP

Welcome to this sleep guided meditation

Called **Rainbow Power Body and Power Animal Sleep**

Let's begin

Here is the opportunity to energy cleanse and aid a therapeutic dream

What a wonderful way to go to sleep

Please prepare your pillow

Refresh the pillow by simply and quickly squeezing it

Let's make yourself a dreamy pillow

Please lie down your whole body

In the bed now

Head soft onto your pillow

Closing one eye to begin to connect inside

Closing the next eye to begin the magic

Are you ready to listen and follow me?

I shall teach you to create a wonderful rainbow body

And also the magic of meeting a lovely power animal

To aid sleep and dream time

Let's enjoy this

Please place your hands on your heart

Your heart rainbow colour is

Green

Now command and tell it to spin, faster

Tell it to cleanse and open to great love

Let's breathe into green and blow out green air

Please place your hands now on your throat

Your throat rainbow colour is

Light blue

Now command it and tell it to spin, faster

Tell it to cleanse and open to great power

Let's breathe into light blue and blow out light blue air

Place your hands now on your belly button

Your belly button rainbow colour is

Yellow

And command and tell it to spin, faster

To cleanse itself and open to great wisdom

Breathe yellow in and blow out yellow air

Place your hands now please on your forehead

Your forehead rainbow colour is

Deep blue

Command and tell it to spin, faster

Tell it to cleanse itself and open to a great imagination

Breathe in deep blue and blow out deep blue air

Place your hands now just below the belly button

Here just below the belly button is your rainbow colour

Orange

Command and tell it to spin fast

Tell it to cleanse itself and open to great order

Breathe into orange and blow out orange air

Now place 2 hands at the top of your legs, on the hips

Your hip rainbow colour is

Red

Command and tell it to spin fast

To cleanse itself and open to a great life

Breathing into red and blow out red air

One more rainbow colour

Place both hands on top of your head

Your top of the head rainbow colour is

Purple

Command and tell it to spin fast

Tell it to cleanse and open to creation the big universe

Breathing in purple and blow out purple air

Let's continue with your rainbow body

And move the body into a star shape

Stretch fully out your arms, your legs, spread like a star

Feel a tiny stretch like a shooting star

Make a wish if you please 1 2 3

Stars are magnificent and aid sleep time too

And now welcome a big, gigantic cleansing of the whole room

Magical flames of violet fire

Let this magic fire clean up the bedroom you are in

Magic, magic flames, dance in violet flames

And everything is super clean and tidy so fast

Time to enter your deepest relaxation with something special now

Let all the body deeply relax, get comfy

We will bring in a lovely power animal

For they are great friends, very wise and exciting too

You have in fact, many power animals that love you through life's journey

You are free to decide what power animal you wish to meet at this moment

You may change to another power animal next time too

Or even reconnect to an old, loved pet

So smile, with your eyes, your face, as you allow one to pop in your head

I shall give you 15 seconds to choose, let's keep flowing

It really is time to dream now

Let's invite your power animal to enter your sleep time

And dream time

Have a wonderful new dream together

Sleeping and dreaming magical

Sleep well

With your power animal

And dream

dreaming

DRAW WHAT YOU SAW

IN **RAINBOW POWER BODY AND POWER ANIMAL SLEEP**

A VISIT TO THE MAGICIAN OF WISHES

Welcome to this guided sleep meditation

Called **A Visit to the Magician of Wishes**

Let's begin in your bedroom

Please prepare your pillow, to make it nice and fluffy

Give your pillow a good squeeze now

Then settle into bed

Rest your head, softly onto the pillow

Closing your eyes and let the eyes inside

Go left and right, left, and right

Then up and down, up, and down

And round and round

Then settle the eyes to relax

Squeeze the muscles now, of the right side of the body

Squeeze the muscle too, of the left side of the body

Then relax all the body

Pat your heart lightly, 3 times with your hand

Pat your head lightly, 3 times with your hand

Really want to make some special wishes

So you best seek the magician of wishes

He's a very tiny magician

Though his hat grows a little, from time to time

He lives with nature and with the animals of the magical forest

Time to pay him a visit, through dreaming of course

So start dreaming

So see yourself spinning around 3 times

Thinking, I must seek the magician of wishes

Listen carefully

A friendly old black crow, comes into view

And beckons you to follow him

Out into the countryside, step by step

But soon a stray horse is spotted in a field

Crow signals, to borrow the horse for the rest of the journey

By circling above it

As you grab some carrots, from the soft soil out in the countryside

You call the horse to be friends and ask politely to ride him

Opening the gate and quickly bond to the horse

By giving this horse a name

Because that's what animals like us to do, to feel special

And introduce your name too

Crow is excited, as you mount the horse and gallop faster and faster

The wind blows lovely onto your face and body

Crow flies always in front of you

Prompting you to turn left and right

Feeling strong and alive

And up into a most enchanted magical forest

Nature is big here

So very colourful, as you head closer to the place of the magician of wishes

What is really magical, the closer you get, the more magical you feel

As you ride together as one

The huge trees seem to bend and sway, opening up a clear path

The long wild grass gets smoother

Then with excitement, the crow makes an unusual noise

As you break to stop and catch your breath

And watch crow land on the most unusual, interesting tree

Absolutely huge, this tree

That looks like it has a big face upon it

Its trunk seems to have 2 large round eyes

A small nose and a large mouth

It makes you smile

Above this face are some animal shapes

A large dog's head

And a full shape of an owl

You look straight up at this tree, and you cannot see where it really ends

Almost forever to the sky

Then crow comes to rest upon your shoulder

His soft deep eyes, fill you with calmness and a little excitement

Now someone is burning a real fire, for long thin smoke rises steadily

It is the magician, whose home hides deep in this great tree

It's time to climb down from the horse and walk up to the tree

And spin around 3 times now

Saying, "Help me please, magician of wishes"

Now instead of a door opening

A bridge is lowered with a big white arrow, pointing to follow up the bridge

The horse trots along with you

As you walk on this bridge

You notice a snail is stuck in the side of the bridge

So you decide to help the snail and lift it to safety

Then a faint buzzing sound, on and off and buzz, buzz

A bee appears on the bridge floor, looking tired and hungry

So you pop the bee onto a wild flower, to get nourishment

Then lastly, a stray cat, very small and black, sees you

But looking a little frightened

So you beckon it over for a stroke

Of befriending this little black cat

At which the little cat gladly decides to join you for company

Now the bridge comes to a round door with a silver bell

So you ring the silver bell and wait

The magician of wishes, opens the door very slowly

A very small magician with a tall, pointed hat

Looks at all of you for a full 10 seconds…

He is able to see your heart is wonderful

He nods at the horse to go and shelter and rest with the other animals

And quench his thirst

Then he welcomes you in for refreshments

And to sit by his fire

But also to grant your wishes

The little black cat loves the fireside

The crow feels very much at home

As you drink a long fizzy drink

Almost magical drink, you start to feel

So happy and very dreamy

The magician of wishes, tells you with his bright eyes and face and a tall hat

To tell him in one breath what you are wishing to happen

So take that nice deep breath and let the magician write down your wishes now…

Everything

Goes very bright and sparkly as he takes the paper of wishes

And throws them all onto the fire

He encourages you to deeply relax

By the warmth of the fire

Feel your face warming and glowing from the dancing flames of the fire

And dream all about these wishes

After all, it is the right time and place to do it

And see yourself in this big dream, the wonderful things your heart desires

And make it sing

For when we truly focus on our wishes

Then the magic happens, making wishes come true

Remember, you are in good hands of the magician of wishes

As you dream and dream

Bring your wishes alive

Be close to them now

Sweet dreams

Dream

Big

DRAW WHAT YOU SAW

IN **A VISIT TO THE MAGICIAN OF WISHES**

THE DREAMWORLD OF LOVED PETS

Welcome to a special meditation dedicated to your animals

Called **The Dreamworld of Loved Pets**

Let's begin

In your bedroom

Please squeeze your pillow, make it nice and fluffy now

And into bed for dreaming

Please lie down and deeply relax

Closing one eye for you

Closing the next eye for your pet

Gently tap your heart 3 times with your hand

Wishing to visit your pet in their new place

The dreamworld of loved pets

When things like this happen

One thing is for sure

We still love them

We still think of them

So we can create a dream and be with them

Let me take you to that dream

There is a certain journey to get there

And other children are missing their pets too

Have just joined a queue

Waiting at a bus stop

But not for a bus

But for a long pink and blue dragon who helps all children

To go and visit their much loved pets

All you need at the bus stop

Is a clear picture in your mind of your much loved pet

The long pink and blue dragon has already picked up other children

And they are smiling with dreamy eyes of meeting their pets

Up in the dreamworld of much loved pets

Look, listen and feel the wind blowing on your face

For a really long dragon of pink and blue is stopping

At the bus stop in front of you

He opens his door, to the seating area up on his long back and long tail

As he checks, you have a clear image of your pet in your mind

On top of the long dragon seating area, there is a faint smell

Of really all those smells pets did have

When they were with you on earth

Can you smell it?

There is a feeling of such great love of soon, so soon to meet your pet

All children are holding onto a smile that belongs to them

And that special one they are thinking of

The pink and blue dragon has filled all his seats

And announces with a fiery, pink and blue long breath

"We are all going up straight up now

Sky high over the clouds,

Over the rainbow

Over the sun

Over the moon and stars

To the dreamworld of much loved pets"

Great flashes of light and speed of a pink and blue long dragon

Transports all of you to the dreamworld of loved pets

Arriving on time, to begin in a way your new adventures

As you all stand up now and make your way out

Don't forget to stroke the dragon

And say thank you and pick me up later if you please

All the children, plus those who have been here before

All head to the first stop of the complimentary Pet Store

For treats and toys to pick before the visit begins

All you have to do is show a clear image in your mind at the Pet counter

To collect complimentary free treats for your pet

Like their favourite snack and favourite toy

Now take yourself to sit in this nice picnic place area

Now the picnic blankets are simply magical and do hover just a little

And tend to pick you, as you walk through this colourful land of dreams

As you step up onto the picnic blanket that has chosen you

It pops out like magic a complimentary picnic box

For you may wish to have a little something yourself, during your visit

So seated, make sure your hands are free

Put your pet things onto the magic picnic blanket

For in this special place, special things will begin to happen very very soon

All pets here are looked after and have family here too

But wish to comfort you and start new adventures together

Simply spending time together

To enjoy hugs

To enjoy picnics in this dreamworld of loved pets

Talking and listening to you

To let them know what you have been doing

They still think about you and watch over you

Get good at creating some new happy times here

Take in the colours, the wonderful adventure land

Where being here will fill you back up with love

So many children and so many pets will have holidays here

It's time to hold the image of your pet in your mind

Pat your heart lightly 3 times

And call their name 3 times, loudly in the mind to come and join you now…

Your pet should come straight to you now, for love is everlasting

Friendship is always remembered

Enjoy now this special place, special things

So I wish you both and bless you both

Sweet, exciting, wonderful, amazing dreams together

Exploring making new memories together

Keep dreaming together

Enjoy your time together off you go now, have your adventures

Sweet dreams

DRAW WHAT YOU SAW

IN THE DREAMWORLD OF LOVED PETS

CHERRY BLOSSOM FUN

Welcome to this guided meditation

Called **Cherry Blossom Fun**

Let's begin

Please get comfortable seated or lie down if you wish

Closing your eyes thank you

Hold the breath please for 7 seconds now

Breathe out cherry blossom

So cherry blossom does come from the tree itself

Let's connect to a cherry blossom tree

It's good if it's twice your height

So you may now walk under its umbrella of pink blossom

Get an instant pick me up of sheer bright pinkness

A glowing pink light

Begin to spin

Spin yourself around

And watch a blur of pink circle energy fill you up

Keep spinning as millions of cherry pink blossoms become

One with you

Breathe energetically into it all

The fresh floral scent

Be captured upon its light pink vibration

Imagine now a strong fresh wind

Grabs your attention

Blowing into your face

Tossing your hair

Deepening your breath

In that split second the wind

Releases all the pink cherry blossom

Feel a soft shower of pink rain, pink petals

Over your head your shoulders and into your aura too

Bonding to a vibration of sheer happiness of natural beauty

Look long with your eyes and wait

For all the blossom in slow motion to land all around your feet

Connecting, looking down to the lovely pink ground

Feel a comfort of standing only with this tree

Have some fun now

Wish for all the fallen cherry blossom

To be drawn to your living vibration

And magically attached re-attach to yourself

In a way you have become a cherry blossom tree

It feels good to radiate such loveliness

A sky high vibration

Feel the feet want to grow roots into the earth

Let the roots run deep and wide into this life giving soil

And the more you truly ground, the more you stand tall

Feel a rise in perfect balance

And thank this tree you first met

Feel you have learned something from this tree

Full of lightness

And cherry blossom fun

Thank you

Open your eyes

1 2 3

DRAW WHAT YOU SAW

IN **CHERRY BLOSSOM FUN**

I INVEST IN ME

Welcome to this guided meditation

Called **I Invest In Me**

Let's begin

Please sit comfortably

Take any position in the chair you wish

Bring one hand to the forehead

Say to yourself

I shall focus for the next 10 minutes and invest in me

Relax your hands now

Closing one eye just because you can

Hold the breath still please for 7 seconds now…

Feel the breath long and smooth

Then close the next eye thank you

Using your imagination the mind

Imagine now the beginning of a thunderstorm

One big sky full of black clouds

That seem to throw heavy, heavy rain

A powerful big thunderstorm

And you are sitting in the middle of this storm

Normally you wouldn't want to be here

Yet thunder and lightning is happening all around you

Sky angry rain drenches you

Flashes of lightning, white bolts of electricity

All you can do is identify this is a real thunderstorm

And you identify it is you right here

You begin to realise

Only your true self can stay here

Intend this thunderstorm to dramatically cleanse all your energies

Everything that belongs only to stagnation and has been draining you

Runs away in complete fear of this big thunderstorm

Because only love will stay with you throughout this storm

The louder the thunder, the more you empty and clear your lowest of energies

As you connect right to the centre of your heart

Listening to your heart beat

Perfectly one hundred percent

Here you feel the emotion of your unbreakable love vibration

The thunderstorm disappears

As you rest snuggly in your heart centre

You feel its life force

And life for everything in this lifetime that has touched your heart for the highest of good

Lives here

Nothing else can

You begin to rewire yourself back to the heart

From the vibration of your heart centre

Every part of the body and head fix back into position

All leading to your heart centre

This itself is electrifying

As you, in a way, become now the powerful thunderstorm

You feel loud and powerful

A strength of love its electric current

Runs all over the body and the head

It's a feeling one feels

When something amazing has just happened to you

Feeling so lightning light

That the feet hardly touch the floor

Jumping through the air, the ground like a thunderstorm

The heart telling you it's OK

To feel great, no matter what

And choose to bond and to honour your heart centre

And live on its high vibration

Electrifying connection

Because life looks and life feels better held in the arms of your heart

For in a way everything I have

Someone else has produced and made for me

This is my abundant heart high energy vibration

Because I am now connected, rewired back to my heart centre

Feeling full of thunder

Feeling full of lightning

Feeling and knowing my heart does sing and I listen

I invest in me

Breathing in my thunder

Breathing in my lightning

Exhale I invest in me

Breathing into your heart centre that connects to all the body and mind

Let's awake to the count of 3, 1 2 3

Eyes opening, eyes fully open, please drink some water soon

Blessings and thank you

DRAW WHAT YOU SAW

IN **I INVEST IN ME**

STRESS RELEASE

Welcome to this guided meditation

Called **Stress Release**

Let's begin

Please be seated with feet touching the floor

Closing your eyes

And with your imagination the mind

See stress as a dense energy

Energy that is heavy

Wanting and wishing

To drop all heavy energy stress to the ground

Decide to do this

Drop it all fast

And enter the ultimate of hitting the ground

Breaking it all down

For everything above is your life force energy

This belongs to you

Anchor your roots once more

To the centre of earth

Breathe softly into your roots

Then place your hands across

Left hand to right shoulder

Right hand to left shoulder

Squeeze tight both shoulders with your hands

Then slowly move the hands

Slowly down the arms over the elbows

And down to the wrists

And meet palm to palm

Focus on these hands touching, supporting each other

Place the palms on your lap now

Feel this position is perfect to start afresh

Connect to your true self as pure energy

Feel a rise in your posture

Chest moving up

The head rising a little

And softening the face

And breathe into newness

Let this newness be smothered in new energy

And this new energy is white energy

That hugs all of you from head to toe

Like an energy white robe

Take a slow breath in and let this whiteness

Travel deep into your mind

Feel the face is shining brightly

Brighter and brighter

See yourself spinning

Spinning around and around

Full of lightness

Building up a clear vibrating life force field

That is positively singing of lightness

Acknowledge your true self

Ready to continue life with great energy and passion

Focus now on the top of your head

Feel a crown of golden light sits you firmly into the chair now

Golden brightness glows all around your mind

As you radiate a crown of golden light

Raring to flow once more with life

The importance of your own things to do

Say to yourself

I am ready to flow

And brightly move about in this energy field

I feel great to be full of lightness

I love the golden shine upon my head, my crown

I love that I am wrapped in energy whiteness

I am dressed ready for action

Getting back to everything with new fresh eyes

And my sparkly golden crown

And my robe of lifting light energy white

I love my golden crown

I love my white shining robe

My body loves the sparkle of bright white

I am ready for action

I am ready

Breathe deeply into golden

Exhale golden light

Breathing deeply into white

Exhale white light

I am ready to flow

I am ready

I am ready to flow

And brightly move about in this energy field

I feel great to be full of lightness

I love the golden shine upon my head my crown

I love that I am wrapped in energy whiteness

My white shining robe

I am dressed and ready for action

Let's awake to the count of 3

1 2 3

Eyes opening

Eyes fully open bright

Please drink some water soon and thank you

DRAW WHAT YOU SAW

IN **STRESS RELEASE**

ANGEL TIME

FOR MORE ENERGY MORE POSITIVITY

Welcome to this guided mediation

Called **Angel Time for More Energy More Positivity**

Let's begin

Lie down fully for this one

Or at least fully supported in a comfy chair

And closing your eyes thank you

Hold the breath for 7 seconds now…

Feel the breath long and smooth

With your imagination the mind

See the room you are in transformed into a brilliant white room

Your room flooded into whiteness

Bathe yourself in this lovely white room

Feel its strong connection to peace

And an invitation for angels to visit you

And focus now please on grounding yourself

Think of the feet that walk the earth

That keep you grounded and physically balanced

See the souls of the feet of left and right

Begin to grow energetically new strong roots into Mother Earth

Sending your roots to the centre of earth

Breathing in, I wish to anchor my roots that say I am here

Be in a state of peace

So that the angels can with ease, fully enter into your energy field

To work with you and support your desired outcome

Bring your thoughts to wishing to connect to powerful angels of love and light

That the process is in fact deeply therapeutic

A wonderful experience

Let's expect this to be a beautiful personal meditation

See yourself connecting, a strong desire to have more energy in your life

And with more energy comes more positivity

Feel your entire self, entire being getting ready

For the angels of love and light will enter soon your energy field

To manifest your desired outcome

And that after this meditation, there may be signs to nourish you self in new ways

That will support truly having more energy and positivity

Let's relax you more now

Connect to lightness

Feel the face soften

The body deepens into peace

That you are open and ready

For a very personal angel of light, to come to you

All there is to do now is ask and give permission

Breathe in gently and slow

And getting ready now

Gently breathe slowly

Relax into your deep serenity

That opens you up for angel time

Breathing in, my angel time

Connect deeply to these words

I wish, with all my heart,

With all my mind and earthly body

To welcome in

Angels of love and light

To empower me with more energy and positivity

I wish, with all my heart,

With all my mind and earthly body

To welcome in

Angels of love and light

To empower me with more energy and positivity

I wish, with all my heart,

With all my mind and earthly body

To welcome in

Angels of love and light

To empower me with more energy and positivity

And now all I can do is let you totally trust and receive this divine energy

Have a full 10 minutes, be truly open to all these angel energies

Blessings and enjoy

(10 minutes for the magic)

Breathe in

Breathe in angel light

Exhale angel light

Breathe deeply your angel light

Exhale your angel lightness

And thank you, to the angels of love and light

For this energy healing received

May life be blessed with more energy and positivity

Keep the faith

Please connect to your roots into earth

Breathe in, I am grounding to earth now

Let's awake to the count of 3

1 2 3

Eyes opening

Eycs fully opcn

Have a gentle stretch

Put a smile on your face

Please drink some water soon

Thank you and blessings

DRAW WHAT YOU SAW

IN **ANGEL TIME FOR MORE ENERGY MORE POSTIVITY**

HOW BIG IS THE WIND?

Welcome to this guided sleep story meditation

Called **How Big is the Wind**

Let's begin

Begin this story in the bedroom

Please prepare your pillow

And squeeze it tightly

Make a dreamy pillow

Settle into bed

Get really comfortable

Closing your eyes tightly shut

Eyes are ready for dreaming, all night long

Listen for the wind

On a windy day and on a windy night

Soft sounds fills my ears completely

It feels good to feel the wind so close to me

Full of lightness

It reminds me too of being in the shower

So clean and soft, water always is

And so is the wind, clean and soft, very fresh

My invisible playful friend, it is the wind

Wind is big, possibly the biggest thing in the whole world

It likes to touch things and move them about

From the ground, all the way up to the highest of clouds

So first I investigate and look down to my feet

At green grass, so tiny, each blade of grass

That makes a fresh lovely playful green carpet, so soft

But wind makes it sway

All individual blades of grass, in many directions

Leaning to the left as if bowing to the wind

Grass leans to the right, for the wind is in a hurry

Then I look up, sky high

And clouds are bopping along on the wind

Time for some cloud staring

Cloud gazing can be fun, for it makes me feel different but good

I stretch my eyes high

I can almost feel the clouds, that move on the wind

Makes me think and see the whole world is truly spinning

Gravity keeps my feet on the floor

So wind has a lot of fun with clouds

Making them big, making them small, and extremely fluffy

Between the green grasses and all those clouds

Leaves, 1 by 1, drop softly on my head and at my feet

Wind runs through trees looking for anything loose

Now autumn, the wind plays a game of leaf dropping

Catching you out, of course

All my clean clothes from the washing machine hang outside on big windy days

Mothers love the smell of wind on their clothes

For it smells so fresh and airy

But hanging washing out makes me think of sails

That move ships and little boats faster through, yes, wind power

Set sail as huge fabrics catch all the air, pushing the ships and little boats forward, yes wind travel

What about the sea?

Succumbing to the wind with ripples and huge waves

For nothing is still but dancing, big style

Side to side, up and down, and around and around

What about the birds smothered in feathers?

And feathers are so light, the perfect combination for wind

Air currents, wind currents, and large flocks of birds

Will travel from country to country, called migration

How else can a bird reach the tallest of tress, without wind as their companion, their friend

And back to me, for I am not a cloud, not a bird or a tree

But wind runs all around me and through me

Touching and tickling me, feeling very alive

Goes up my nose, before I can think

Looks down my mouth and throat into my tummy

Runs through my fingers and thumbs

Tosses my hair

And every tiny hair on my skin

Is pricked up by the wind

My eyes feel the pressure, as wind looks me in the eye

The temperature means wind has been to many places

Arctic winds may visit me, so cool and fresh

That my breath turns to white fog

Or perhaps a hot wind, of Mediterranean heat

Loosens my clothes and I crave for shorts and T shirts

What about wind beyond the earth?

Into the universe, all around the planets

For it is invisible but touches everything

If I blow out now, my breath, my air

Am I not the wind inside of me too?

For I feel it, as I blow my breath on my skin

A little wind, but still the wind

Can the wind send me to sleep?

Be soft, be gentle and sway me so quietly

So I can drift into dreams

I shall follow wind into my dreams and play like you

Dreaming something special, about you

And something special, about me

So as I fall to sleep, let wind lift my feet off the ground

Feel the wind, under my feet

Let me travel by wind and see more and more different wonderful things

Although I am human, I think I could fly and float on the wind

Maybe my arms will have 2 giant sails to catch the wind blowing through me

After all, it is a dream

Let it take me and be full of lightness

Exciting to move about like the wind itself

Maybe I will have some fun

Explore and travel by wind

With a smile on my face, let me

Bond and befriend the wind

And dream something special, about you

And something special, about me

Go to sleep now, go to sleep now, 1 2 3

DRAW WHAT YOU SAW

IN **HOW BIG IS THE WIND?**

FESTIVE SNOW FUN DRAGON

Welcome to this guided sleep meditation

Called **Festive Snow Fun Dragon**

Let's begin in your bedroom

Please prepare your pillow

Squeeze your pillow tight making a dreamy pillow

Time for a quick body stress release by simply contracting all muscles inwards

Making a ball of muscle

Then relax, please settle into bed, get comfortable

This snow sleep requires a new dream giant friend that is here for you with blessings

Let's be very still now for the snow dragon to visit you for dream time

It's exciting meeting your white festive dragon but

Must pretend to be asleep, so closing your eyes, do not peek

Eyes shut and getting ready to enter your dream with a new giant friend

The snow white dragon is special

With a huge white heart full of love, of festive winter fun

Anyone can have a white dragon, it's kind of like a present

So now slowly put your hands to rest on your heart

Remember you are supposed to be asleep

Your heart is beautiful and strong

But the heart of a white snowy dragon

Would fill this bedroom from the floor to the ceiling and every wall

Notice and just feel the bedroom is becoming quickly very snowy white

And puffs of white fog from the white dragon's breath fills even your bed

He or she is up to you, do you want a female dragon or a male dragon?

You may make a choice now

Most of all, dragons have fantastic huge wings for flying great distances

Also a huge, long back to ride upon when you have made friends of course

The heart is white as snow and beats like a big drum

And your little heart beats like a drum in reply

Hearts love to beat like a drum

Dragons prefer, because they are so magical, to be named with just a number

Because numbers are cool

The reason for the numbers is because there are millions of white snowy dragons

That wish to bond and befriend the young hearts of children

My dragon is called number 82

Numbers are fun and so is your dragon

So pick your number now if you please

So let your heart be open and listening to your big festive white dragon

Let both hearts beat as one, ready to fly tonight

But first it's time for you to shrink to tiny

So there is as much room as possible

For the white dragon in your bedroom to flap open the flying wings

When you are tiny you are so light

So think tiny and light and shrink to super small

The smaller you get, the brighter you shine in the night

Dragons love your shine and hear your heart like a drum

Let the dragon have a good stretch and open his fantastic flying snowy white wings

Which should take 30 seconds from now so please wait…

Time for you to sparkle and shine so the white dragon can see you in the night

Think sparkle, think shiny

Blowing out huge white foggy breaths, your dragon captures you within it

And now you float up out of bed and onto the dragon's back

Secure and seated nicely on the back, peeking out for direction to fly

At the count of 3 your dragon will boom up high

Like a rocket to the night sky

So 1 2 3 and boom

Enjoy the ride going up

Up and straight to the snow clouds

Big ones full of snow of course

Now snow is really millions of snowflakes together

Each a different pattern

They sparkle like snowy stars

Time for you both to follow the snow clouds where they need to be

Flying on your white dragon and you shining like a star

Snowfall must happen for this festive time of year

Time to watch everything change from colour to snow white

The world is big, and in some places it's a new day

Time to watch the snowflakes float and float all the way down to earth

Landing in big heaps of snow

This will bring a lot of children out to play and have their fun

Snow sport games will begin too

Many champions will ride down snow hills on skis very fast indeed

But now your dragon wants to give you a very special snow ride

That only dragons can do

And begins to search for mountains

Looking for the perfect mountain top

So higher than the clouds you go, up higher for mountains are giants

Getting closer and landing on a great mountain top covered in snow

With just enough time to make a snowman here at the very top

So jump down and gather your snow and make a great big snowman here

You have 30 seconds to do one now please

And now back onto your white dragon shining like a beautiful bright star

Put a smile on your face and a kiss on your dragon too then a big breath in

For at the count of 3 getting ready to slide all the way down this snowy mountain

It's going to be a long, big snow ride

So ready 1 2 3 and slide…

The question really is

Do you want to do the snow dragon ride again

Or perhaps fly to more snow mountains and more new snowmen to make

Most of all

I want you to continue dreaming

With your snowy dragon, getting closer and closer as friends

And have a good long chat to your dragon

For the big dragon's heart is open and listening to you and your festive wishes too

So dreaming big and fun now

Decide where to fly next and what snow games to do together

Just enjoy your snowy festive adventure

Keep dreaming together

May your love and friendship be bright as white snow

So goodbye and goodnight to you both

DRAW WHAT YOU SAW

IN FESTIVE SNOW FUN DRAGON

THE COMFORT BLANKET

Welcome to this guided sleep meditation

Called My Comfort Blanket

Let's begin in your bedroom

Please prepare your pillow

Squeeze it tight make your pillow fluffy and so very light

And fully into bed now

Closing one eye to sleep

Closing the next eye to dream a special dream

About the fantastic magical comfort blanket

That comes with blessings

So rise into a smile

For it is simply magical and is filled with the greatest of love

Natural beauty, super protective and empowering

The comfort blanket is like the magic flying carpet

Although it looks almost square and thin

It can do so many happy wonderful things

Think of the world, all of it, how big and colourful the world is

For the comfort blanket is made of all of this

So wishing for the comfort blanket to come to you

It almost can hear you

Calling and calling for it to come and comfort and support but also to enjoy

Send out a message saying I am here, I am in my bed

Comfort magic blanket come to me now and fill me with wonder

Waiting 10 magic seconds

1 2 3 4 5 6 7 8 9 10

Then imagine floating down from the wishing universe

Onto your entire bed, a blanket that flies and floats into your bedroom

Almost smiling and loves to be here right here for you

Although it is almost square and thin it is so bright

It shines like all the sunshine captured inside of it

Connect to a rich glow of lightness so light, a feeling so high, exciting and fun

And it lands on top of your bed

It immediately chucks out anything that's heavy

So if your head feels heavy

Then goodbye to heavy

If your body feels heavy

Then goodbye to heavy

It is very much a working blanket that is beginning to connect you to deep comfort

Now it captures you in its lightness

Anything good can happen now

It begins to show you wonderful things that you love

Such a worldly blanket too and loves to show you many wonderful things

It presents a miniature forest sitting upon your magical blanket

As you look closer with wonder, great reindeer are softly moving through the forest

Rabbits so super soft pop and bounce, sniffing the air

The squirrels run up to the tallest of trees

Little green frogs hop to the sweet lazy river

Then the magic blanket becomes a long thin lazy river

Watch the fish sway and swirl and bubble along the happy river

A forest dragon is drinking from this river and sees you looking at him

The dragon is full of adventure and wants to show you and share some time together

Simply nod your head and exchange a smile

For the forest dragon loves to help children feel special and extremely happy

This brown and green forest dragon lowers himself flat to the ground

So you can step onto his comfortable back

Then a little hug is all he needs to take flight

Watch your comfort blanket, magical blanket, turn into a sky of white clouds

Up and off you go together

He wants to find you a blue crystal to bring back and put under your pillow

To give you more magic powers

So he is looking from the sky for the crystal caves

Soon a strong energy of crystals shimmers and glows from the earth

As your dragon flies straight down to the most beautiful enormous cave

The entrance is full of diamond crystals

But he is looking for the special blue crystals

That are perfect for children and a perfect size for putting under your pillow

The blue crystal is perfect for children and understands comfort and fun helps them

To sleep perfectly, encouraging more wonderful dreams

So you must jump down from the forest dragon and walk into the crystal cave

Keep both your heads low looking closely at the ground

As soon as you see a blue pretty light then you have found the right type of crystal

Everything is shining and shimmering in the crystal cave

Put your hand over the first blue crystal you see and ask very nicely

To come home and live with me

That you want very much to have a blue magic crystal under your pillow

This should magically loosen the blue crystal from the cave floor

And sit on your hand wrapped with your fingers and lots of love

And now come out of the cave ready to fly back all the way home

But please enjoy this for it's fun to fly and have a new dragon friend

The forest dragon really likes to be back in the forest

And takes you there first

He's got a little itch on his back that he would like you to scratch

It's a bit like a tickle and he appreciates your help

Watch your dragon smile as you do a great job with a tickle and scratch

He then reminds you of your comfort blanket

And he points to a big green field

A very square field almost the same shape as a blanket

For your comfort blanket as turned into soft grass

With curly and very woolly sheep springing about on this green meadow

The little blue flowers pop out of the grass, warmed by the sun

More and more blue tiny flowers appear, they smell wonderful

Then you remember your blue crystal is still in your hand

Remember the forest dragon told you to put it under your pillow

To help you to support and comfort you

Making dreams more magical and fun

Let the blue crystal get comfortable

And the more comfortable the blue crystal gets

In your new home, your bed, your pillow

The more colourful the bedroom becomes

It begins to glow a wonderful blue colour all around your head, magic blue

Breathe in the colour blue

It feels really nice and relaxing but also exciting

It tingles all around your pillow

It then makes all the bed tingle with joy and happiness

The feeling so light it is simply sending you to sleep

The best sleep is feeling incredibly light

So I wish you goodnight

DRAW WHAT YOU SAW

IN THE COMFORT BLANKET

THE WOODS

Welcome to **The Woods** guided meditation

Please get seated or lie down if you wish

Closing your eyes and let me take you

To the woods

For the hidden magic of nature

That touches the heart

Hold your breath still for 5 seconds

1 2 3 4 5

Breathe and connect

I need to get out

But it's got to be to the woods

I need upliftment, I need to feel good

And bring my body and mind, back into brilliant balance

The heavenly home is turning into a box

All 4 walls north, south, east and west

Have sealed me in

And it feels stagnant

And the air is thin

I need a break, for my mind and body

Bring a voice together, ringing loud and clear

They're both telling me, to get out of here

All chores have become a bore

It's all lacking satisfaction

No matter how much I complete

For I need to put soil and earth, under my feet

I need to trip over stones and slide in mud

Press new grass and leave a print

I need to walk away from this manmade world

I can't breathe deeply enough

And the eyes to my soul have lost their sparkle

I need to connect to the woods

To the seasons that are pushing forth

I want to see flowers wild and free

Patterns of leaves

I need to walk amongst the tallest of trees

I need to walk without time and whistle a piece of grass

A trick I learnt, as a tomboy lass

I need high pitched sounds, of only the birds in song

Under the biggest umbrella of trees

No sound of traffic at last

It fell off my shoulders when I left, the concrete path

I need to forget about the treadmill of life

I need a break as I'm not feeling right

I need deep earthy oxygen pumping in my veins

And simply be

Born again

I want rosy cheeks, that I had as a child

I want to pick a nice long dry straw

And stick it in my mouth

I want to get excited at finding the perfect walking stick

And snap it to a desired height

Striding from the feet

I need to catch sight of woodland birds

Or see a rabbit, truly bouncing about

Gaze long into the distance, at the chance of seeing a deer

And feel its peace

I want to suddenly hear cuckoos, penetrate the air

With that unmistakable sound

That cause my ears to bend a little bit more

I want mud on my shoes, like a dirty dog

I want to wash grass stains and twigs out of my hair

I want to see 10 shades of green

As far as the eye can see

I want a sky that's going to seduce me

I know the patterns of nature are easy, therapeutic to the eye

And green is my heart chakra colour, for all of us

And my eyes fall heavy on millions of heart shaped leaves of green

I want to put my index finger under a raindrop

Suspended from a desired leaf

Because it's clear and pure and good enough to drink

I want to stare into a spider's web

And let my eyes get hypnotised, by its brilliant deadly patterns

And let out a sigh and cause it to quiver

I want to squash fallen berries, under my feet

Kick a crab apple and watch it roll with speed

Down a long muddy lane

But most of all

I want to rest my back against a nice solid tree

One that will outlive me

And run my fingers through blades of soft grass

Rest my head fully back

And roll my eyes high

And show only the sky

I need to see the sunshine put on a display

With sparkle rays, exciting my eyes

And watch the shadows run away

I want to hold sunshine in the palms of my hands

I want to smell the good earth

I want to smell the plants

I want to open my ears to every sound of nature

I'm weighing myself, checking in

That mind and body have returned to perfect balance

And have I come back to my roots

Before I leave here, I've already booked in again

As I should

My subconscious mind

Will tell me in time

I need to get out

But it's got to be

To the woods

Thank you

And it's time to open your eyes

Stretch and feel alive

DRAW WHAT YOU SAW

IN **THE WOODS**

3 GIRLS 1 UNICORN

Welcome to this guided meditation called

3 Girls 1 Unicorn

Sit comfy or lie down if you wish

Let me tell you a story

Close your eyes thank you

Once upon a time a unicorn helped

Mr and Mrs Jones and their family

Mr and Mrs Jones have 3 children

They are different

But then again not

They are triplets, a set of 3 girls

They looked the same

But didn't act the same

At the age of only 8, something big did happen

It was great news for one, Sally

Poor news for another, Molly

And bad news for the third, Jilly

They found out their father would lose his job

And be forced to only get part time work

The 3 girls loved already many things in life

Sweets and toys and holidays

The first one said

"Oh no I will never have as much fun

For it costs money to buy things I like"

The second said

"I will hold onto what I've got

And settle with that

No point in expecting things to get normal again"

The third felt a strong fear wash over her

Then realised the power of change

If she used that energy for good

When they went to bed that night

They all dreamt the same dream

They started on a journey spreading the news

Of their father's loss of job

Being replaced with part time work

They got 3 main reactions

But they also said ask the unicorns

First was shudders of bad luck and hardship to come

And warned them to prepare to tighten their belts

For they would be going without many nice things

Or you could ask the unicorns

The second opinion was a hint of change for the better

For the new job may lead to full time

If he does a good job and keeps smiling

Or you could ask the unicorns

Thirdly was how much quality time you will have

With dad watching you all grow up

More family time

Maybe you can work for yourselves too

Thinking as a team together

Or you could ask the unicorns

The truth is, dad wasn't happy in his full time job

And therefore didn't do a great job

He was ready for a change

He was missing his children too

He looked forward to showing his children

The wonders of the natural world

And hobbies that just may be more important than money

To just keep spending

The unicorns were still on the triplets' minds

And decided to ask what the future holds

So set the intention to meet one

Legend has it unicorns only come through your heart

When dreaming and only then can you meet one

When fast asleep in bed

All 3 girls held hands to fall asleep

And soon their thoughts led them to dream the same dream

They stood together all in front of a large gate door

They looked at one another to check it was the same dream

Then opened up the gate

With a white mountain in full view

And so began the journey

Up the white mountain to the land of the unicorns

The mountain path was full of white flowers everywhere

Shining like lights

Their eyes opened wide at the endless waterfalls

Of frothy white water and huge rainbows inside them

That seemed to beckon them to refresh their tired feet

But the more they carried on the better

And lighter they felt

They began to believe in the magic

A golden tree caught their eyes

With a heavy load of golden apples

Of which they began to eat one each

And because they love animals

They put one each in their pockets

For the unicorns too

Finally on reaching the top

They stood waiting to see what would happen

In the distance they could see a herd of unicorns

So bright the light was beautiful

Beyond words they could feel the magic

Something told them to wait right there

For unicorns must always approach you first

They remembered the golden apples

And cupped them each in their hands

And lowered their eyes listening

Everything went very bright

For the sheer whiteness of these unicorns

Has the highest of great magic about them

Speaking directly to their hearts

They told the unicorn their concerns for their father

And the family and the future

Touch my unicorn horn for it grants wishes

Of the best of the best outcome

They glimpsed their future of extreme

And exciting things to happen

Where new ways of living life successfully

Doing great things that involved the natural world

The creativity, the hobbies, the natural talents

Would create a secure loving family home

Suddenly the golden apples began to jiggle

In the hands as each was eaten by the unicorn

Invited for a ride, a flying ride of sheer fun

So snuggly they all 3 sat

As the unicorn that galloped so fast his wings did open

Far and wide and lifted them all up high reaching the clouds

Shooting stars danced over all their heads

And wished to keep always happy

Like a unicorn naturally does

A shower of rain filled the air, magic rain

That simply made them laugh so much

That laughing tears rolled down their red hot cheeks

They continued to circle the white mountain

And saw it was in a perfect white heart shape

Glowing magnificently

All the time they sat on his back

Their hands lovingly stroked and squeezed

Hugs of excitement

Whilst riding and flying

The unicorn was also healing them

And continued to speak to their hearts

For the very best outcome I can reveal to you

A new future is to begin

Where nature trails, writing, poetry, dancing,

Astrology, learning languages, reading endless books

The list was endless of things to do and fill their lives

With more happiness and more satisfaction

It was now time for the unicorn to fly them home

For it was time to lay the triplets back in their beds

Asleep of course

When morning came

The triplets looked at one another and talked honestly

"Bad news is it, Jilly? "

"Poor news is it, Molly? "

"Great news, Sally? "

"Are you still sad about this bad news, Molly? "

"Are you scared full of fear, Jilly? "

"Can you see it going anywhere, Sally? "

Then they all said together, "No,

I mean yes, we are happy for dad and us,

We will have a great adventure. " 3 big smiles were on each face

"We will have a great adventure, our family"

The end of this story please begin to open your eyes now thank you

DRAW WHAT YOU SAW

IN **3 GIRLS 1 UNICORN**

I DREAM OF FAIRIES

Welcome to this guided sleep story meditation

Called **I Dream of Fairies**

Let's begin in your bedroom

Please squeeze your pillow

Make your pillow fluffy and fairy light

Into bed now

Rest your head

Onto the dreamy pillow

Getting very comfortable

It really is time to dream and connect to fairies

Because they are the best kind of friends to dream all about

So closing one eye to dream

Closing the next eye for fairy friends to begin

Let the eyes inside go round and round

Round and round

Like you were watching a fairy fly all around your head

They are so tiny, so light

Let the eyes rest now, for dreaming happens when we rest completely

Time to begin

Listen to your heart, for it loves so many things

And loves the tiny fairies full of big, big magic

They are colourful and cute to look at

And really quite clever, making everything fun

Fairies create a lot of excitement and adventure

For everything in this world looks gigantic to them

Through the eyes of a fairy is like looking at the world as a big jungle

Living and flying in a very colourful big, big jungle

A blade of green grass is like a tall green tree

Being super tiny gives fairies access to go everywhere

The biggest thing about them is their fairy wings

How wonderful it would be to have fairy wings too

So think now of your back

Feels a bit empty, doesn't it?

And plenty of room on your back for wings

To magically be made

For how else can you travel to fairyland

To be amongst fairy friends

Concentrate and focus on your back

Wishing for your own wings

How many wings do fairies have?

Is it 2, is it 4?

What colour are they?

Pure white or pretty colours or perhaps completely clear

Breathe into your heart a smile as you become so light

Just thinking about fairies

And fairy magic makes your heart so very light

So begin to believe

You must believe in the fairy magic

The power of believing will take you to fairy dreams

Soon, very soon to fly out of this bed up and up to the world of fairies

But your body needs to be so very tiny no bigger than a fairy

Time to magically shrink

So smaller and smaller

Keep wishing to be smaller

And believe it is happening

The power of believing in fairies is the answer

Tiny hands, tiny body and your wings a little bigger than you

Then let the air all around

Become magical air

And capture you in a bubble of air

Making you so bright and magical

This magic bubble with you inside

Floats upwards now so very light

And waits for the wind to take you on this journey

Befriend this wind and politely ask for a ride to fairyland

Let your wings move and flap in the bubble of air and ride on the wind

It's time to go now

Keep bright

Please hum or sing to yourself for fairies love the sound of singing children

To sing is to hear the gift of your beautiful voice

They are listening to your happiness

Getting closer to fairyland

And of course closer to fairy trees

So flying and riding over the big smiling moon

Bouncing over fluffy clouds, one or two

Winking at the stars

That seem to wink back

Time goes quickly

Arriving in the land of magic

With special magic trees

That are absolutely loved by fairies and all animals

The fairy trees

The tallest one here has a door upon it

It looks like a fairy secret door

Looking closer now, for that door that invites you to stay a while

Find that door with welcome to fairyland

Please enter a small room for your visit must be recorded

Written in their magic book

The date, the time, your name of your visit

And what you want to do and learn here

For fairies love to learn something new each day

They are lovingly connected to nature and to animals

As you stay here for a visit you will need to copy them

And have a good drink of magic honey

As soon as you drink it the golden magic honey

Then, only then, are you ready to fully go around with the fairies

The honey drink is bright and yellow, almost golden

And makes you glow golden bright

Well I hope you enjoyed that special drink

Time to step out of the door and smile with your face

Smile with your heart

And smile with your fairy wings

In your bright beautiful bubble

You are ready now to join in

Making the most beautiful fairy ring

The ring represents friendship

They know the power of being a good friend to each other

And each shall listen to you

And you shall listen to the fairies

Sharing everything they see told in stories

Anything new they have learnt that day

A lot of celebrations

And they are grateful for all the beautiful things in this world

Let the wind fill your wings and your bright bubble of air

It's time to have some fun looking through the eyes of a fairy

For keeping all things fun and light enables them to fly

Remember a fairy can go anywhere into the cracks of any door

Through anything, really

Every flower has a soft springy bed

Swimming laughing and floating on leaves down the tiniest of streams

When you look through the eyes of a fairy

The outdoor nature is big and powerful and always enjoyed

Each fairy comes of course with magic

This is connected to their own magic bubble

They simply live and go everywhere in their own magic bubble

To keep safe and protected for only love and lightness can enter

Which makes them clever too

Can you feel your bubble of air around yourself?

For it makes you glow so very bright golden bright

Fairies collect a lot of information here

By talking and listening and looking at everything around them

And share all their adventures of what they learn each time

So would you like to help the fairies and learn about something new?

Time to grab a fairy friend

Or If it's your first time, let someone pick you right now

Smile with your face, your heart, your wings and bow at your fairy friend

Then you can learn something new

When you both find something new

Perhaps a baby tiger, a cub?

Remember they love animals

Just smile with your eyes together

Connect to this sleepy tiger cub

Of all the things a little tiger must do to be what he was born to be

Drawing what you see is also popular

So begin a new fun learning adventure fairy style

Tell all your fairy friends later in a story

So you are learning about all creation

Feel free to pick anything you are curious about

Just remember to smile deep into their eyes

Off you go now and dream so very light

And share it with the fairies

When you all sit down, all together

Making the most beautiful fairy ring

Drink some more golden magic honey

And each will listen to you

Perhaps the story of the tiger cub

And you will listen to the fairies

So I wish you a very exciting colourful dream

A fairy adventure

DRAW WHAT YOU SAW

IN **I DREAM OF FAIRIES**

DOGS DREAM JUST LIKE YOU

Welcome to this guided sleep story meditation

Called **Dogs Dream Just Like You**

Let's begin

Please prepare your pillow

Squeeze it tight for great adventurous dog dreams tonight

Get comfortable into bed now

Let's connect and bond with the most famous animal of all, the dog

Please close both your eyes just like a dog does

Let the eyes inside go round and round

For dogs when sleeping move their eyes too, dreaming of course

They seem to have great adventurous dreams

Feel your lips puffing with air breathing into a new dream

If only you could move your ears like a dog

For they seem to twitch a little when fast asleep

Relaxing your eyes now

Make sure you are as comfortable as a sleeping dog

Now we know dogs love to run and run so fast so very far

Let's go and catch up with a favourite dog of your choice

See yourself running up to a friendly dog

Decide if this dog is yours or a new one you most definitely like

Because you are dreaming, you may find you can understand each other well

So before the big adventure why not have a mini picnic here

Something to eat for you both and something to drink too

I shall leave you both half a minute to do this now enjoy…

Have you noticed how much all dogs love to meet and greet everyone they see

They love company and playing about

Physically they are big explorers

With a great nose that smells everything around them for miles and miles

So your dog really wants very much to tell you some amazing things about being a dog

First, it's true all dogs really do dream

Because they spend their quiet time sleeping and that means dreaming too

Dogs have a good reputation and can be most definitely the best friend ever

They provide endless entertainment and relax into family life

They are great company, no matter what you are doing

They lower our stress levels

They help us sleep better because they are masters of sleep and dreaming

Their loyalty holds no bounds

All dogs feel emotionally close to us

They love to make eye contact for they love to bond with you

All dogs understand gestures like when you are pointing

And learning tricks by listening to your voice

Now some are indeed working dogs, yes, working dogs

That have a beautiful family history that runs through them known as breeds

Such as the border collie, the poodle, the German shepherd

The golden retriever, Doberman Pinscher and the Shetland sheepdog

Working dogs with physical and mental gifts to help people

Remember these are dogs that are good at guarding things

Or pulling carts and sleighs

Performing water and land rescues and assisting blind people - the list is endless, really

Now a deep breathe in ready and it really is time to begin an adventure together

So a long adventure ahead, for it's time for this dog to visit their old mum and dad

Who live in a different place

So a big bark fills the air, sound moves on the wind

Then waiting to see if anyone replies

So please wait 10 seconds...

The fantastic hearing of your dog receives messages

Did you hear anything yourself?

Then your dog sniffs the air very deeply for 10 seconds now...

So much information can be smelt that helps to give direction to go

It's time to start running and of course jumping over anything that is in the way

Keep smiling like a dog who's just heard his favourite word

Walkies

Now very soon after all that running, you both stop to drink lots of water

And also to ask other dogs about the dad and mum you are both looking for

Remember when puppies are born it is very exciting and the news travels far amongst all dogs

Because they know often puppies will not see them again

Although this is natural for all dogs to gain a new set of human parents

Then you both realise even mum will live somewhere else and the dad also

So please continue this journey in this adventure dream and find both

And share some great stories of what everyone has been doing to stay happy and strong

Keep running and dream together

Go seek, go find your dog's proud mum and proud dad

Dream big and adventurous and happy

DRAW WHAT YOU SAW

IN DOGS DREAM JUST LIKE YOU

DREAM BETTER

Welcome to this guided sleep story meditation

Called **Dream Better**

Let's begin

Into bed thank you

Fitting the pillow snugly to the neck and head

For this pillow will support a great dream tonight

Make sure the body is covered and smothered in your personal bedding

Closing one eye to sleep

Closing the next eye to dream better

Each night we enter this personal date with ourselves

This precious night-time to reboot and repair all of you from head to toe

Let the eyes inside go round and round, round

As you lie here you also lie on Mother Earth

As she goes round and round spinning and creating gravity

So you are supported by her she loves to keep you grounded

For your journey on Earth

Let the eyes relax now

Let's resolve any restless tension in the energy body

Your energies are made of yin and yang

So by leaning into the right side of the body

Tensing tightly a few seconds, now the right side

Connecting to my male yang energies

Breathing into my male yang energies

And now leaning into the left side of the body

Tensing tight the left side for a few seconds

Connecting to my female, my yin energies

Breathing into my female and yin energies

Relax into balance

Let's create easily and quickly a white space to encourage sleep and fun dreams

Simply imagine all bedroom walls turning into white

A blank canvas of white

Switching off from the physical world of physical life

Breathe into whiteness

And the floor below turning white

Then the bed the pillow and everything touching you dissolving

Into soft white, powerful and cleansing

Breathe into your private white space

The body loves the pampering of newness

We are creating the meaning of brand new

That will reflect on a new day, a new date in the morning

Now imagine looking up to the bedroom ceiling made of glass

Revealing instantly a huge night sky

The night sky is so deep

So royal deep blue in colour

Connect to it by

Breathing into deep blue and exhale the colour deep blue

With this the movement of white clouds drifting so very slowly, yet drifting

Cloud gazing begins

Offering at first nothing but peace

You are observing the movement and flow of everything above you

Stars everywhere

That shine and shine just keep on shining into the eyes of your soul

Dreaming must happen it must be fun

It is your right to feel good right now

The fun dream truly refreshes the mind and boosts life to flow

Now something is coming soon to offer a big dose of fun

For already looking up to this vast universe that touches the night sky

Are you ready to be connected to real dreamtime fun?

For there is a part of you that knows no limits to your dream imagination

So like great news out of the blue

What is coming to you?

For it's made of the night sky

Here is a very free flowing high vibration

It is made of night clouds the illusion of shape shifting dream making

And made of stars that are extremely bright and intelligent

Time for better dreams for personal fun and experience to be connected to you

A gigantic mystical fun creature full of divine love and wisdom

With a vibration so high

But you must meet it half way

By first emptying your mind completely for 10 seconds now thank you

And once more empty your mind please for the final 10 seconds now

Breathe into a dream companion of a high dimension night blue dragon

Remember life has changed a lot on Earth

The dragons of higher dimensions are returning to Earth in abundance

To assist humanity to live in the new golden age of great joy and abundance

They have powerful loving hearts, great wisdom

Thus they act as personal companions to lift our vibration

So trust and believe for the meeting

Of your personal night blue dragon of uplifting dreams

Is coming to connect and collect you

Therc's going to be a big fun dream tonight

There are no limits, no discrimination, no cancellations

Just pure power flowing with lift off

Reaching as high as you can imagine

But a night blue dragon can imagine a whole lot more

This is a gift, a great tool in life, for dream time should be fun

So the sky begins to refocus into a night dragon

This deep blue sky becomes its body

Feast your eycs on a huge deep blue night dragon

With dream making white clouds breathing out of his nose and mouth

Absolutely beautiful, calling you to great fun dreams

The dragon's eyes are full of stars, bright and intelligent

Lifting your soul into divine peace and enchantment

He is the perfect dream companion

And all he needs to know to connect is your name

So let your heart tell him your name now...

It really is dream fun time lift off

And scoops you up with such speed and excitement

Freedom to dream bigger begins right now

The night blue dragon

Who has absorbed your name into his heart

Takes flight with you fully connected and straight away off somewhere great

To a brilliant energetic new planet to detox and rejuvenate you

Before the big fun dreams begin

Feel free to be pampered so precisely here

Detox is essential to keep your vibrations high and clean

Take kindly the first offering of a drink here of this deep energising potion

That is presented wrapped and held in a shimmering crystal cup

Drink it up, put into your body this present, this tonic potion drink

Let it hydrate and support all of your wellbeing

Only goodness may enter your supreme being, after all, you are made of love

It's good to feel good, let it work wonders

And a shimmering giant waterfall of the same potion is pointed at

For you and your night blue dragon to go under

Let your eyes fill up with the abundant size of this high vibration waterfall

Time to let off some steam too and get a little excited

Imagine singing your heart out

Being joyful and being silly and express all your emotions right here

So I shall leave you for a minute to do this and enjoy...

The night blue dragon is all about fun, being a great tonic in life

And is creating a deep friendship with you just by being together in this moment

A great power animal, mystical of course

And in a way is your new aura friend and support

Now this energetic planet has been a great start

And recognise a shiny new feeling about you

Time to move on and let the night blue dragon fly

And fly and find some more fun

You have choices and a gentle nudge here

Would you like to see and experience another new destination?

Another high vibration planet perhaps

Maybe you would like some higher guidance on your life path?

For there are many wonderful minds out in the great universe

That want to support you for your highest of good of course

So that would take your night blue dragon flying to the left

The left side of the body

Or would you like to visit a dear old friend who's moved away or moved on from Earth?

Or visit an old family pet from any year you can think of?

That would take your night blue dragon flying further to the right

The right side of the body

Remember you have free will that is limitless and creation itself

Indeed you can do both to fill this great dream

Remember you are in safe hands of your night blue dragon

And arrive smiling wherever that may be

Your choice to go left first or go right first

And don't forget that the new morning, a new date

To feel that sparkle is still with you

So dream big tonight, dream fun

Trust your dragon companion

Will take you and you shall be enlightened and enjoy it all with blessings

Have fabulous fun so get busy living get busy dreaming dream fun tonight

DRAW WHAT YOU SAW

IN **DREAM BETTER**

WELCOME TO YOUR INDIVIDUAL JOURNAL – LET'S DO THIS!

WHAT AGE AND HEIGHT ARE YOU NOW?

WHAT FRUIT AND VEGETABLES ARE YOUR FAVOURITES?

171

WHAT FLOWERS AND BIRDS ARE IN YOUR GARDEN?

NAME SOME OF YOUR FAVOURITE BOOKS.

WHAT MAKES YOU SMILE BEFORE YOU EVEN DO IT?

WHO DO YOU LOOK UP TO?

173

WHAT DO YOU LIKE ABOUT MUM?

WHAT DO YOU LIKE ABOUT DAD?

174

HAVE YOU ANY SISTERS OR BROTHERS? PLEASE TELL ME ABOUT THEM!

HAVE YOU ANY PETS? PLEASE TELL ME ABOUT THEM!

WHAT WOULD BE THE PERFECT BIRTHDAY PARTY?

WHAT WOULD BE THE PERFECT HOLIDAY?

WHO ARE YOUR SUPERHEROES?

DO YOU KNOW ANY JOKES?

HOW WOULD YOU DESCRIBE YOURSELF?

PLEASE DRAW A PICTURE OF YOURSELF.

DID YOU KNOW SMILES KEEP YOUR HEART MUSCLE HAPPY

AND KEEPS YOU PRODUCTIVE? SO PLEASE DRAW LOTS OF SMILES NOW!

WHAT DO YOU DO AT WEEKENDS?

WHAT IS YOUR FAVOURITE SUBJECT AT SCHOOL?

LOVE AND BLESSINGS TO YOU - DRAW ME A LOVE HEART THANK YOU!

About The Author

Born in North Lincolnshire 1966, Linda Owen comes from a large Yorkshire family of seven children. A nature lover by heart, Linda dabbles in poetry. She has entered a personal journey of self-help through holistic therapies and then became a practitioner, a Reiki lady and a natural born storyteller. Her writing has taken on many forms, ranging from different topics of books with the themes of wellbeing, spiritual, poetic and even humorous.

Linda is now working as a meditation teacher on the global website – Insight Timer, with lots of guided meditation stories and although originally for adults, now caters for children too. Her acquired knowledge through time and her age has brought more life wisdom to share.

With her background in holistic therapies, this enabled Linda to get her work (since 2020) out verbally, online and in audio style, benefiting others, covering a wide age group of people who are interested in the holistic approach of natural wellbeing of the mind and body through guided meditations. Then it occurred to Linda that it would be lovely to put all the children's stories together in a book, to enjoy a new experience and become a useful tool to aid sleep time and wellbeing.

Her stories are tender, magical, all about promoting a positive mindset through a positive creative imagination, proving that sleep time may be wholesome, nurturing, and empowering.

https://linda-OWENs-website.yolasite.com/

https://insighttimer.com/lindaowen

Amazon reviews welcomed.

www.blossomspringpublishing.com

Printed in Great Britain
by Amazon

16992359R00108